*

Being &
Journey

By

J.J. Bhatt

ISBN:

9798857627884

Title:

Being & Journey

Author:

J.J. Bhatt

Published and Distributed by Amazon and Kindle worldwide.

This book is manufactured in the Unites States of America.

Recent Books by J.J. Bhatt

HUMAN ENDEAVOR: Essence & Mission/ A Call for Global Awakening, (2011)

ROLLING SPIRITS: *Being Becoming* /A Trilogy, (2012)

ODYSSEY OF THE DAMNED: *A Revolving Destiny,* (2013).

PARISHRAM: Journey of the Human Spirits, (2014).

TRIUMPH OF THE BOLD: *A Poetic Reality*, (2015).

THEATER OF WISDOM , *(2016).*

MAGNIFICENT QUEST: *Life, Death & Eternity,* (2016).

ESSENCE OF INDIA: A Comprehensive Perspective, (2016).

ESSENCE OF CHINA: *Challenges & Possibilities*, (2016).

BEING & MORAL PERSUASION: *A Bolt of Inspiration*, (2017).

REFELCTIONS, RECOLLECTIONS & EXPRESSIONS, (2018).

ONE, TWO, THREE... ETERNITY: *A Poetic Odyssey, (*2018).

INDIA: Journey of Enlightenment, (2019a).

SPINNING MIND, SPINNING TIME: *C'est la vie*, (2019b).Book 1.

MEDITATION ON HOLY TRINITY, *(2019c), Book 2.*

ENLIGHTENMENT: *Fiat lux*, (2019d), Book 3.

BEING IN THE CONTEXTUAL ORBIT: *Rhythm, Melody & Meaning, (*2019e).

QUINTESSENCE: *Thought & Action,* (2019f).
THE WILL TO ASCENT: *Power of Boldness & Genius,* (2019g).

RIDE ON A SPINNING WHEEL: *Existence Introspected, (*2020a).

A FLASH OF LIGHT: Splendors, Perplexities & Riddles, (2020b).

ON A ZIG ZAG TRAIL: *The Flow of Life*, (2020c).

UNBOUNDED: An Inner Sense of Destiny (2020d).

REVERBERATIONS: The *Cosmic Pulse,* (2020e).

LIGHT & DARK: *Dialogue and Meaning,* (2021a).

ROLLING REALITY: Being in flux, (2021b).

FORMAL SPLENDOR: *The Inner Rigor,* (2021c).

TEMPORAL TO ETERNAL: *Unknown Expedition,* (2021d).

TRAILBLAZERS: *Spears of Courage,* (2021e).

TRIALS & ERRORS: A Path to Human Understanding, (2021f).

MEASURE OF HUMAN EXPERIENCE: *Brief Notes,* (2021g).

LIFE: An Ellipsis (2022a).

VALIDATION: The Inner Realm of Essence (2022b).

LET'S ROLL: *Brave Heart,* (2022c).

BEING BECOMING, 2022d).

INVINCIBLE, (2022e)/ THE CODE: *DESTINY,* (2022f).

LIFE DIMYSTIFIED, (2022g) / ESSENTIAL HUMANITY, (2022h).

MORAL ADVENTURE, (2022i / SPIRALING SPHERES (2022h).

EPHEMERAL SPLENDOR, (2023a) / CHAOTIC *HARMONY,* (2023b).

INTELLECTUAL MYSTICISM (2023C)

WILL TO BELIEVE (2023D)

EXPECTATIONS & REALITY, (2023E)

THREAD THAT BINDS (2023F)

ONCE & FOREVER, (2023G) PERPLEXED, (2023H)

GO BEYOND (2023i) / BEING & JOURNEY (2023j)

4

Preface

Being & Journey is an indefatigable adventure; reaching out directly to the core essence of young minds. Indeed, it is the attempted journey of their self-awareness, their authentic identity and of course, their endless possibilities to change the world toward higher inspiration, hope and overall harmony than their elders who failed to act efficiently in their gifted time.

Let the collective young, "Global Spirit" grow. Let it glow and let it actualized their big dreams; lifting Humanity above all. Let them make the world inclusive, forward-looking and open-minded with a moral confidence. Let the young braves boldly declare, "We're the unified historic force in-making, and ready to pass on the torch to the succeeding generations to sustain the integrity of the mind, *what they ought to be."*

J.J. Bhatt

Contents

Bold
Journey

Drop brooding
And begin reasserting,
The Self with your
Endless possibilities

Don't run, but
Be bold to stand your
Moral ground and be
A hero of the time

Enough of
Bickering, conflicts
And senseless violence's
And wars

Leave them
Behind and be the
Force of positive change
To the troubled world

Yes, be the
Mover and shaker of
Humanity, and fearlessly
Save it that you must…

Eye in
The Storm

Living
In the world,
Swirled by the
Nasty storm

Where is the
Escape to be free,
And move on for a
Greater meaning

Not enough
To be simple and
Passive, but be a
Self-confidence

Keep ascending,
And dare save
The fading hope
And dream

No point;
Suffering, just take
A bold stand, and
Be the winner while
The journeys on…

Roll
Back

Creative Soul
Not just an ordinary
Artist, but an endless
Imaginations bursting
On the scene

All there is
Nothing, but shining
Awakened beings holding
Curiosity to unveil secrets
Of the mystical universe

Meanwhile,
It's high time to resolve
All the insanity of the
Corrupted mind and
Misdeeds

Let him rise up,
Let him wake up and
Be fearless to roll back
The spiritual track…

Trials &
Errors

Just
Walk through
This passage of
The dark tunnel

Now,
Is the time
To keep steady along
The rough path

Don't run
Away from the dark
For there is light at the
End of the tunnel

Young braves,
Just stay steady and
Know well,

"Being human
Means, to walk
Along a highway of
"Trials & Errors," and be
Triumphant forever…"

Turning Point

Being
What a de facto
"Universal Image"
Itched with endless
Challenges indeed

So, let's
Reckon,
" The journey shall
Not be a free lunch"

Know well,
We're the core
Essence

Not for any
Esoteric knowledge,
But for the wisdom,
"How to lift humanity
Above all"

Let's grasp
This simple truth and
Keep the journeys rolling
As one mighty positive
Force at every turning point.

Toward Perfection

Let every
Being be inspired
To be a lightening
Rod

Let every
Freaking being
Wake- up from
His deep slumber,

And shake-up
His thick layers of
Vanity and greed

Yes, to
Transformed to
Be good and take
Responsibility

To change
The world from
Violence to be
Peaceful, and
From being selfish
To be a selfless love…

Global
Task

We shall
Endure always
Through whatever
The challenges we may
Face either today or
Tomorrow

We're
Here to ascend from
Trivialities and senseless
Tribal claims of divine or
Whatever that may erode our
Moral strength

Let's
Keep rolling toward
A meaningful shining
Path, and

Do something
Good for billion others
Who're dying from hunger,
Violence and wars…

Being &
Truth

Love,
That's first-hand
Immortal experience
Of life to be

To purify
The journey of the
Soul while the time is
There

Once
In the lapse of
Eternity, love turns
Into something of a
Greater meaning,
That we don't know yet

Indeed,
Earthly love is the
Best beginning where
Deep feelings reverberate
The entire cosmic rhythms

So I say,
"Let's fall in love
While we ride through this
Emotional human form…"

Time to Wake-up

Time to
Transcend from
Troubled humans to
Be enlightened beings

It's only
Such awakened spirit
Got the power to change
The world for good

Remember,
It's our collective
Sheer ignorance that's
Been exploited by the
Greedy few

Time to
Be aware of
False narratives,
Preaching's and the
Blind worshipping

Be smart to
Know the stratagem
Schemes of the
Powerful few of today…

Mission
To Roll

What the
World need is a
Durable unity to be
Free from this asinine
On-going conflicts

Let us
Erase racism, terrorism
And the gluttony of the
Ever threatening AIs and
Whatever else

These
Super hi-tech trends are
Undermining our moral
Endeavor to bring "Good"

Folks,
Time to dismantle
The "House of Insanity,"
And catch-up with the
Mind-set of the
New Dawn; beginning,
Today…

Love

Love
Blooms the best
When lovers grow out
Their trivial fights,
Silly show-offs and

Evolved being
Enlightened souls;
Seeking
A deeper meaning
For a common destiny

Love,
Ideally expresses,
When two souls
Understands,
"What is their genuine
Humanity at the core"

Let love
Evolve from earthly
To the heavenly bliss at
Every step of the way, and
Be the lovers forever...

Awakening

While we
Still enjoy our freedom
To think independent of
The super-smart –
Machines

Let's
Remember well,
"We're the
Inheritors of moral good
And Rational goodwill, and

We do care
For the dignity of our kind
And the Planet Blue"

We still
Desire to save our
Family warmth, our security
And a better future for our
Kids

Yes,
We're deeply concern
With the negative forces
Hanging over our heads like
A Democlise's sword…

Journey

Honey,
Don't rush to the
Commitment of
Love

It's a long
Journey before
We can utter,
"We're in love"

Honey,
Please try to
Understand,

"Love is not
Cheap like throwing
Old pairs of shoes"

Love is a
Sacred vows and
Must embattle at every
Breaking-point

With an
Iron-clad trust and a
Life time commitment.

Nova Prayer

Let there
Be a new dawn,
"Where creativity,
Compassion and
Confidence be a norm
Than an exception
In every heart"

Let there
Be a new mindset
Powered by the
Integrity and fearlessness;
Driving every human
Toward future called,
"Global Goodwill"

Let such an
Awakened spirit inspire,
Soul of every concerned
World citizen,

Let it be
The daily affirmation of
Every responsible being
Of the twenty-first …

Self
Truth

What if
We're half 'n half
Male and female
Subspecies of our
Kind

Only when
We merge;
Manifesting,
"Love, compassion
And truth"

We're
Half 'n half in
The state of suffering
And happiness,
Rationality and
Irrationality, and

In
That stubborn
Old mode,
"We live and die
At the same time..."

Déjà vu

H.G. Wells
Saw it well over hundred
Years ago in his famous
Book, "The Time Machines"

His time travelers
Had to wait eight-hundred
Thousand years to witness,
"Human devolution"

His envisioned,
Interaction between two
Kinds: Eloi (the capitalists)
And Morlocks (factory workers)
Was a big time biz venture
And went on for sometime

Meanwhile,
Morlocks kept working
Like the slaves; concomitantly
The Eloi became lazy consumers and
Dependent upon their sweating slaves

Well, in time,
The Morlocks became
Aggressive and began to call the
Shots while the Eloi learnt their
Biggest blunder, but it was too late
To turn the tide in their favor?

Our Time!

Sadly,
Those who were
In powers,
Failed to change
The future of the world
As they cared for
Self-interests and greed

Here we're
Today where the
World is heading toward
Full of techno-superiority
And leaving helpless
Humanity behind

There is
Endless conflicts either
Openly or behind the scene
While the serious existential
Issues are getting worse

All the big talks
By the elites, all the
Shibboleths by the guardians
And the preachers seems
Empty words, and of course
Lack of sense of emergency of
Our time...

Life
As Is

When
We're alive,
We're somebody
We're the limelight
We're the propellers
Our dreams

Indeed,
Being alive,
We're the curious
Beings willing to
Play the game to win

Alas, the time
Mercurially slips away,
And we're not the same
Who we're once

As end nears,
Loved ones, friends and
Everyone slowly fades
Away from the scene

Only memories
Keeps life going for a
While, and suddenly,
We're no more, but only
The image in the frame
That hangs on the wall…

Insanity to Humanity

"So what,
If the world is going
To the dogs?"

"So what,
If the war keeps
Million dead?"

Well, that's the
Rhetoric's of losers
Who don't understand,
The value of humanity,
In its total sense

Every human,
Must grasp moral
Responsibility

To save
The Planet and life
Yes, to leave a world of
Purpose for the children
And theirs to come

Let all
Narcissists, solipsists
And the cursed seven sinners
Be reformed and return to
Their normal state of sanity...

Forever

Don't
Bow down
To anyone, but the
Self-truth

Don't
Be obsequious
To others, but be
The self-confident,
That you must

Don't
Listen to the,
"Nay sayers," for
They're not the real
Friends

Keep away
From toxic people,
But stay with those
Few who nourishes
And inspires you
For greater missions
In life that's so brief…

Nothing, But Love

I feel
Your total love
In your tears and
Smiles

I notice
Your total love
In your jealousy and
Deep concerns

Oh yes,
I experience your
Pure love in all your
Sacrifices

Love, love
What an omnipresent
Magic ever since we
Kissed,
For the first time…

Sooner
The Better

That's the
Way, life rolls forward
Sometimes
It's rewarding with
Fulfillments of all dreams,
And sometimes, mercilessly
Not

Against,
Such an uphill battle,
Each must get smart and
Begin the steep climb with
A strong will to reach out
To the highest peak

Nothing is
Given free and easy to
Most struggling beings
That's why,
Wake-up, arise and be
Serious from the beginning
And know the script well…

Naked Truth

In romance,
There is exploding
Passion and intensified
Emotions

In time,
The magnitude of
That high temperature
Slowly abates

As the
Romantic illusion
Fades;
Upwelling feelings of
Doubt, betrayal and
Guilt

Love
Never a quick
Experience
There is something
Magic called,

"Mutual
Trust, respect
And a quick sense
Of forgiveness..."

Introspection

Often
History tells us,
"Human alone is the
Ridiculous error"

He's been
A vacillating half-
Animal throughout
His existence

He has
Known only, "How
To make it and destroy
One civilization after
Another"

In modern
Age, he hasn't forgotten
The old habits and the
Monumental struggle
Continues,

"How to be
An enduring moral being
And build a better world…"

Profile

Let's
Take a glimpse at
The veritable mirror
Of our collective self-
Profile

It reflects,
Our few good deeds,
And many misdeeds
Since the beginning
To date

We also see
A complete absence
Of our intricate
Virtuosity while

Riding through
This jungle of
Misunderstandings,
Ignorance and arrogance…

Flipside

Wonder,
What is a genuine
Essence of my own
Being?

I mean,
What's the
Meaning of my
Coming to this
World?

Is it,
Just to live a life
Of struggles, tears,
And guilt only?

Why
End-up in such an
Overwhelming
Existence

When
I am trying to
Roll toward my
Real identity!

Expose´

Why let
Religious dogma
Turn humans without
A love or soul, but pure
Hatred toward others

Why they
Perpetuate
The opposite of the
God who stands for
"Good of the whole"

We're
Intelligent beings
And we carry a sense of
Morality and justice at
At the core

Why then
Fall for such false
Preaching's and be a
Bleeding animals
Powered by
Hatred, violence and
To a point of total insanity
In the twenty-first?"

Rage

It's in you,
I believed our love
To be forever

And, now
You've crossed
The line of no return

How can
You forget the dreams
We held together once

How can
You forget, inspiration
We'd for ours to come

It's over,
It's over forever
Let's
Forget this charade,

And move on
Separately
For another better
Tomorrow elsewhere…

Off the Cage

Why
Weaponized,
Divine
For political
End or to take
Revenge; gaining
Nothing in return

Why
Crush young girls
Of their dream by
Imposing the
Outdated belief

And, why kill
Innocent by standers
In the name of insane
Claim; gaining nothing
In return, but hate

Isn't it
Time to be refined
And logical humans and
Gaining your respect in
Return?

Zealots

In holy water,
God placed the seed of
Intelligent beings to be

Perhaps,
To deliver His divinely
Wisdom to the world

Once,
The holy bottle fell
In the hands of a few
With malicious intention

There began
All our troubles as
Humanity
Turned fragmented,
Deeply bloodied and the
Sinners; controlling the
Narratives

The Divine is
Petrified as He witnessed:
Hatred, violence and wars
Being justified in His Name,
What a shame, what a shame,
Indeed…

Proclamation

We're
The expression of
Consciousness while
Passing through this
World of fascination

We're
Universal theme
That constantly
Flows through
Light and dark reality,
We know it so well

Let there
Be either highs or
Lows, we don't
Care

Let there
Be right or wrong;
Testing our judgment,
At any time for

We're the
Creative minds on the
Move to understand,
"The Self Truth."

Gratitude

Thanks
To a few great
Historic heroes

Who took a
Bold stand against
Those
Instigating mass
Destructions and
Deaths

Thanks
To those brave hearts
Who held their
Grounds

To save humanity
From complete
Extinctions, time
After time

Let us,
Salute "Global
Heroes;" fighting to save
Our dignity as children of
One Maker, time after time"

The Game

Human
Weaves experiences
Of courage and passion
To illuminate his
Moral vigor

Yes,
That's why
He's challenged to
To be the image of
Goodwill all right

Though
The rules of the
Game are set and
Even the direction
Been defined

It's up to
Him to begin the
Real walk while he
Got the green light…

Capricious

Once, I heard
Her singing the
Same love song,
Every time, I passed
Through her place

I heard,
Calling to join her
Lyrics of joy and
Nothing but joy"

Love,
What a mirage
Of memories only
To be heard in
Dreams

Lovers
Once so nearest,
And now
Many seas apart,
"Love, what a
Mockery to face?"

Inspiration

It's
Rumbling,
Stumbling,
Crazy strolling whims

Flying
Through the
Rough terra of hope
And big ambition

Humans,
Often caught into
An uncongenial situation;
Facing imminent moral
Crash

That's why,
Major great epics:
Mahabharata, Ramayana,
Iliad, Odyssey and others
Do stir-up to gain some
Pragmatic wisdom

Time to be
Inspired and to grasp
The very meaning,
"What we ought
To be, and how to
Triumph over issues
Of our time."

Goodbye

Dear Lady,
Don't hold onto
Your illusion any
More

Please,
Don't think, all
Is going to be fine
Like yesterday

Dear Lady,
I understand,
"Your deep grief and
Willingness to say,
"Sorry"

But dear lady,
It has happened
Million times

I can't take
It any more, yes

I can't be
The victim of your
Endless apologies,
So I bid you,
"Goodbye forever."

The Quest

Intrigued by
The mysteries of
Existence

Is it,
Not a time to
Refine our selves?

Inspired by
The miracles being
Alive

Is it,
Not a time to
Sharpen our thoughts
And actions

Is it,
Not time to
Grasp the depth of
Our core essence

Is it,
Not time to
Ascend from base
Instincts to far above?

Power
Within

Go where
No thought has
Ever emerged

Go where
No love hit the real
Depth of sincerity

In
Other words,
"Be bold and
Be genuine
With your goals"

Let the
World be in flux;
Full of noise, but
Never go off the
Set track

I mean,
Be a free human;
Holding onto your
Very moral core....

Becoming

Time to
Cross the bridge;
Entering into another
New realm

Where
Worldly folks
Worship only
One Truth called,
"Harmony
And Peace"

Indeed,
In the name of
Joy of all, and not
For a select few

Where
World halting the
Imperceptible
Dehumanization

By the
Increasing; thinking
Non-human machines…

Endurance

Only in
Love, there is
An opening for
All possibilities to
Come alive

Only in
Truth, there is
A discovery,
"What is the meaning
Of existence"

Only through
Genuine endeavor,
"Humans can bring
Ideals and reality
Together as one"

Life,
Always an
Open choice between
Myriad opposites:
Right and wrong

Time to
Reassess. Time to
Think twice, and move
On as an enduring
Truth…

Veritable Mirror

So long
Pulses are on,
We remain, the guest

So long,
We're in love,
We remain meaning
To our own world

Well, so goes
The grand saga of
Our temporal rhythms

In such a
Constant disorder
Of fate, only steady
Conscience is the
Real friend

All there is
To be understood
Be the veritable mirror
Where in we must see
Our collective
Beautiful image always…

No free Lunch

Well,
Contact lenses with
Nano chips would
Expand our vision to
An unimaginable level

Full digitization
Of the brain would
Open up to uploads,
Down loads with
Infinite memories,
All right

If we blink,
Robodoc would give
Med advice and same
With many instantaneous
Pleasures and needs

Well,
Every progress has
Its price like the
"Faustian deal," and
That would be our
Human freedom, I guess…

Eternal
Fire

Hey
Dear Heart,
You never left
The world we're
Once

Hey
Sweet Heart,
Have you ever
Remembered,
"We're in love
Once?"

How time
Flew by so soon,
Here we're
Still living
Through yesterday

Love,
What a stubborn
Emotional fire that
Never dies within…

Confession

There is a
Magic in my inner
Being and it's called,
"Spiritual intuition"

It's only
In the silence of
The night; lets me
Travel beyond

That's the
Miracle of being
Born human and 'am
Grateful indeed

That's the
Experience; separating
"I" from the trivialities;
Let me embrace harmony
And meaning

Whence,
The strength of my
Humanity, my dignity…
My clarity while am
Still ascending …

Simple Truth

Perhaps
Moral courage
Requires presence of
Evil in the world

That may
Well be the
Reason, "Why
Humans were sent
To this realm"

All along
History, it's been
Purely an on-going
Battle between,
"Good vs Evil"

Let
Good triumph
Over evil and
Let us be

Free and
Happy at this
Turning point of our
Crazy history…

Clarity
In Order

Indeed,
Art is long,
And life is short,
Ars longa, ars berevis

And still
In such a naked
Reality,

We keep on
Aimlessly rolling;
Whatever
The future may be

That got to be
Our assignment
Being born human

Let it be
Our set
Responsibility,
"How to be winners
In the chaotic world…"

War:
Face of Evil

Protracted
Wars do transform
"Good humans to be
Heartless and disoriented
State of minds"

It has been
Happened for millennia
And still happening today
And will do so in the future

Well that is
The sad, but ignored fact
Of our super busy lives

When
We keep losing:
Our heroes either alive or
Fallen in any war, we
Lose humanity at the
Same time

War, what a
First-hand stares of
Evil before us, but we
Tend to ignore it all, "Why?"

Fearless

When
There is so much
Sun shine and

The zillion
Stars smiling in the
Night

Why then
Walk along
Such a trail full of
Darkness and despair

Why
Put others on
Such a hellish way

Let our
Collective Spirit
Soar high toward
Beauty and truth, and

Let us
Be the worthy
Intelligent beings of
Moral will and be fearless
Forever…

Excelsior

When
An Individual's
Insight often turns
Into blooming
Wisdom

It got
To fire-up the
Million young
In their time

Let them
Be inspired to bring
Positive change to
The waited dream

Let their
Morality,
Personal faith and
Self-confidence

Illuminate
Their genuine truth
While the journeys on…

Inchoate

Sometimes,
We meet a person
Who has lost humanity
As he doesn't got the
Moral substance to deliver
To the world

Sometimes,
We face a querulous
Individual who has lost
Compassion to understand,
"What others are saying"

Sometimes,
We encounter a person
Who's adamant about his
Troublesome belief and
Refuse to open the mind

Sometimes,
We shake hands with
A high-ranking guardian,
And end up listening to
His narcissistic boastalk

Sometimes,
We wonder, "What's
Wrong with us humans,
Why can't we find folks having,
Integrity of the mind!"

Being & Identity

Nothing
Seems to be
Crystal clear in this
Constantly bubbling
Uncertain realm

Yesterday,
We thought, universe
Was 13.7 billion years
Old bag, and today
The number jumped
To be the double

Yesterday,
We thought the
Dark matter was an
Enigma, and today
We think it's made of
One-trillionth mass of
Subatomic particle

Yesterday,
We humans were
Enjoying, "Who we're?"
Today, its AIs telling us,
"Who we should be!"

Time &
Reality

Listen
Folks, life is a
Indispensible gift, and
Meant to flow toward
Whatever is "Good"

This journey,
Be always toward a
Right direction for
Our time is brief, and
The road to fulfillment,
Very long

Listen,
Young mind,
"Be sure to begin
Walking
To your special wish
As soon as you must

Time
To be mindful of your
Thoughts, words and
Choices before you take
The first bold step...

Contextuality

Why go
To the Unknown
Being,

When there is
An urgent need to
Repair our imbecile
Brains?

What is this
Notion of preaching
Sheer speculations and
Guilt?

When
There is a
Dire need to be a
"Good humans" in
This troubled world…

Ascension

Each must
Be his/her own
Meaningful journey

Each be
In-charge of his/her
Destiny

Let each
Strengthen his/her
Moral will and

Move on
Toward perfection
From the half-truth

Once
Awakened with
Such wisdom,

Let them
Ascend the "Global
Spirit to its best."

Truth
As is

Moral law
"Rit" is core essence
Of the Vedic thought

From
There radiates
Five principles:

Dharma, Karma,
Syyaum, viragya
And kshma;

Leading
To Moksha; what is,
Enlightenment

Enlightenment
Enables humans to
Share,

"Harmony, hope
And happiness with the
Whole," and

That is the vivid
Message of the Vedic,
Aka, "Santana Dharma,"
In brief before the world…

Thank you

Life is a
Constant journey;
Powering humans to
Soar toward truth

Life not to
Be dismissed, but
Revered at each
Step of the way

Life is the
Gateway to
Transcend from
Imperfection to
Perfection

Life though
Plagued with myriad
Challenges, it's worth
Walking through it all

Life,
Only the last
Passage from here
To eternity that we
Must know with some
Wisdom…

Be
Smart

Not
Death, but existence
Purifies human soul

Not
Religion, but the
Inner Mind opens
The way

Not
Heroes, but the
Self endeavor is the
Heroic deed, indeed

Don't
Bow down to the
Pretenders: a big
Celluloid star, leader or a
Pious servant

Learn to be
Your own confident
Being and move on…

Love
Forever

Wow!
We're in love,
What a natural sense
Of our destiny to be

So let's
Dance tonight and
Be the winners of our
Unfolding future with
The first touch of
Our hearts

Let's
Dance cheek to
Cheek and let's kiss
For the first time

Come dear heart,
Let it be the seed of
Our permanent memory

As we
Sincerely take our
Vows to launch the joint
Journey called, "Forever."…

Self-Realization

Given
The turmoil's of
Our time: bigotry,
Violence's and wars

Is it not
The moment to
Direct the mind

Toward
Freedom from the old
Habits of our collective
Blunders and sins

Wonder, thus far
Why our religions,
Common-sense and
Asinine policies have
Failed

Time to
Walk away from the boiling
Cauldron, and learn to calm
Down to save the future of
Our children at once…

Reality
As Is

While walking
through this
Otherwise
Heartless world

Be smart
To be aware of
Intricacies of your
Contextuality with
Others

Be calm
To endure through
The vicissitudes of
Life, and

Still be a
Triumphant hero
Of your ride

Just
Reckon, "What's the
Meaning of your coming
To this world in turmoil"

Celebration

Each is
Born to discover
The meaning of
Life on their own

Each is
Divine in their
Possibilities, and
That's their
Justification to
Exist

Let the
Grand journey
Begin with such a
Moral tone, and
Rational insight

Let the
Grand story become
The brilliant light of
Inspiration to many
Million young minds…

Purification

We're
Purified through
Our thoughts, words
And the best deeds

Yes, it's all done
In favor of the self and
The Soul of the whole

That is the
Enlightened highway
To build an effloresce
Civilization

Yes,
That is the
Passage to the world
Of peace, understanding
And appreciation of
All there is

Purification
Of the corrupt mind is
The ultimate step to
Unify great expectations
And reality; fulfilling our
Collective dream, at last…

Unintended Consequences

Being
While on the way
To be folded into his
Own truth

Often,
Gets caught-up into
The world of self
Illusion

As his
Complex character,
Machination and
Arrogant attitude

Fails him to grasp
The intricacies of
Human relationship,

Consequently, he gets
Trapped into the same
Old folly, time after time, and
The historic tragedy continues…

Historic Force

What defines,
An essential being is
The juxtaposition of
Good to evil in him

That's the
Vacillating line;
Shaping thoughts and
Actions accordingly

He can be a
Wave-maker either
For good or otherwise

And, that is
How, the history of
Humans writes the
Script always

That is
How he continues
To ink it accordingly
Even today, and
Will do so many
Tomorrows to follow…

The Orwellian Ghost

It's been
Tendency of
A cult, ism or an
Imperial order;
Curtailing freedom
To think

That's the
Old game always
Wearing new clothes,
From one age to
Another

It happened
In the past, it's still
Happening today, and

Who
Knows may be;
The "Orwellian Ghost"
Is hovering over our
Thick heads already!

The
Grand
Play

It's in the
Intoxication of a
Romance

Two lovers
Burn their intense
Passion; sometimes
For a brief or forever

Lovers
Sometimes make
Sense of relationship,
And sometimes they
Don't

And, sometimes
Lovers become self-
Centered, confused
And end-up taking a
Fatal action too…

Magnificence

When
We're attuned with
Clarity of all that is

We're reborn
As purified genuine
Beings, and

We're ready
To take off to the
Real meaning of
Our journey

That's the best
Way to move from
Ignorance to the very
Experience of being,
"Enlightened"

Indeed, it's in the
Clarity, we become
Calm and alert, and
Understand,
"What is a veritable
Beauty being born in
Human form…"

Courage

It's
The courage
Where human
Got the power to win
Good over evil

It's the
Courage where
Human strengthen
His moral Goodwill

Let it be
Grasped,
Courage is his
Best friend

Oh yes,
Courage
Shows the way
To the brilliant
Light while the
Ride is on...

Reflection

While
Walking along the
Unknown trail

Be sure
To welcome simplicity
And unity that all you
Can

Let it
Be candidly known
By the deaf world,

"Human is
The supreme with the
Power of his ethics and
Rational insight"

Let it be
Also known well,
"Human is the final
State of awareness of
Freedom and the fate of
His kind..."

High Place

Once
Caught by the
Self-indulgences of
A shallow high societal
Mad world

Often it's
Impossible to detangle
One's individuality
From his pseudo-pride

It's
All about
A doubled life style
In the realm of
High skyscrapers

Where
Super rich call the
Shots and rest serve
Them as their masters

Oh yes,
That's the mad, mad
World of arrogance,
Blind ambition and greed
In constant motion 24/7…

Eviscerate

When
A belief is built
Upon lies, deception
And false superiority

How long
Believers remain
Blind to their own
Rational being

When
Guardian's promises
Great things in words
Only,

How long
Followers remain
Deaf to their pragmatic
Moral being

When
AI's and their clones
Keep controlling the
Human mind

How long
Should intelligent beings
Remain,
"Mute to their freedom."

Eternal Spark

Well, well
So we say,
"We're in love, and
Keep dreaming
Night and day"

That's the
Crazy feelings of
All lovers while
Spinning
In the love sphere

Oh yes,
Lovers keep
Singing, dancing...
Kissing night and
Day

Let the
Lovers everywhere,
Keep on singing,
Dancing...dreaming,
Night and day and
Be happy forever...

Commitment

If I love
You
With my full
Heart

Dear Girl,
Remember, "It
Shall be forever"

Be sure
To know,
"There ain't any
Turning back"

That's
The way,
Love must flow
That's the way,
Our destiny be

Oh yes, it's
About commitment,
It's you and me,
And ours to come…

Great Passage

Being
Alive is the best
Joyous experience

Yes,
To be aware of the
Scope and limitation
Of all there is

And,
Be prepared to
Journey alone with
Positive attitude
Always

That's the
Real trail to walk
Through

That's the
Great passage to
Freedom…

Mental Frame

There may not
Be a moral perfection
As such in reality, but

If we're
Inspired by its notion
To do some good to
Others, then it is

There
May or may not
Be a Super Being, but

If we
Aspired to be an
"Enlightened Being,"
In that case, it doesn't
Matter either way

Nice to
Define meaning of
It all from our mental
Assumptions;

Sustaining
Us animals, to be a
Civilized and peaceful
Human beings…

Walk the Walk

Clarity,
Poignancy
And integrity be
The strength of
Every concerned
Being

Who's
Seeking right
Answers to the
Riddles of existence

Time to
Think positive.
Time to
To believe in the
Self no matter what

Time to
Walk with full
Confidence to the
Waiting reality where
"All is always Good."

Pulse of Innocence

It's an
Old bucolic beauty
Where humanity is
Still alive and well

Thank God,
Modernity hasn't yet
Corrupted their hearts

There
Folks don't have
Feelings of dislike or
Violence
Even strangers,
Are welcomed with
A big smile

They haven't
Seen laptops and the
Cell phones, yet

Oh yes, every
Man, woman and
Child still is a genuine
Human; holding on to
Their humanity, all right…

Forbidden Path

Since the
Beginning to date,
Our kinds been
Looking for a rational
Unity to be of a fact of
Deep meaning

Alas,
Each time, we've
Been discovering,
Nothing, but continued
Cacophony, gluttony
And corrupt fragmentation;
Echoing from all corners

As a consequence,
We keep spinning
Into the historic container
Of fear: nukes, Biogerms and
Climate boiled too!

Man,
What a genius and an
Imaginative mind;
Why is he walking through
The forbidden path?

Solace

Perfection,
What an
Idyllic notion
To go after

May be,
A utopian
Adventure to
Explore

Yet, we
Need such a
Crazy whim
To set the
Distant aim

Yes,
To give a
Meaning, rhythm
And solace to the
Monkey mind,
That we own…

Ars Poetica

Poetica,
Just another
Spontaneous
Joy of the human
Soul

It's a
Spinning wheel
Driven by curiosities,
Feelings and creativity;
Querying deeper meaning
Of Life and time

Poetica,
Always an inspiring
Thought, "How to enter
The realm of beauty and
Truth"

Poetica
Always a noble
Passage to the temple
Of enigmas, riddles and
Contradictions and more…

Issue: Existence

How do
I experience best
Of my existence

Indeed,
Existence that's
A double edged
Sword where
Progress and regress
Remain in collision

That's the
Lyrics of grief &
Joy
That's the
Challenge I face

And as I keep,
Walking along the
Serrated trail; yet am
Not afraid to face it all…

Fantasy *vs* Reality

We seems
A melodramatic
Grand voyage

Trying to
Play out our sheer
Fantasy; believing
Its reality

May be all
Emanating from
Our chimerical
Thinking or what?

In the
Totality
Of all that is,

All
May be just
A self-imposed
Assumptions;
Justifying the
Grand voyage
In motion?

Stay
Focused

Never
Sink to the
Hellish state,
"What is a loss of
Will to live"

Never
Quit the scene
Even in ignominy
Instead stay
Calm and keep
The chin-up

Don't
Let the cowards
Hurt your feelings
Don't let
The liar's control
Your thoughts

Be confident
And be the ice under
The heat always…

Pilgrims

We're
All accidental
Pilgrims

We're
On our way
To the realm
Of fulfillment

Yes,
Each carrying
His/her dreams,
And fantasies

Linguistically,
Culturally and even
Ideologically we may
Be different

Yet, we're
All bounded by
One big goal; needing
To wash the seven sin…

Be
Awakened

Don't
Rush to the
Kingdom of love
So soon

For it's
The garden of
Roses and thorns

Be smart, and
Be calm while
Walking through
It all

Don't
Rush to the world
Of perfection
Too soon

For there are
Many
Fires and storms
To pass through
It all…

Identity

All along
My life, I've
Probed mysteries of
Nature, Divine and
Mind

That's
The mission,
I've been on all
Along my curiosity
Track

It doesn't
Matter, if I've been
Either right or otherwise

I've existed
To express
My earthly concerns;
Extending to grasp the
Meaning of

My
Anthrocosmic
Connectivity with the
Holistic realm…

Etiology

If an
Individual
Doesn't follow
Basic rules of civility

Of course,
It would diseased
The entire society;
Turning it into the
Milieu of toxicity

Let the
Guardians take the
First step and relearn
How to self-restrain

Let the
Strong soften-up,
And be a compassionate
Human being for a change

Civility is a
Total harmonious
Experience to build a
Scintillating civilization
From one generation to
Another *ad infinitum.*

Blind
Souls

We're
Inseparable from
Our ambitions and
Dreams

We're
Inseparable from
Our birth, death
And consciousness

We're
The time travelers
Lost in misreading
Meaning of our journey
To the top

What a
Shame it is, though
We're quite intelligent
Yet lacking wisdom

Indeed, wisdom
That would ford us
To the other side,
"Moral Good to the
Whole…"

Off the Track!

What if
We're being
Unnecessarily
Caught up with the
Barrage of

Subjective
Interpretive adventures
Of faith, belief and
Societal grief?

I mean, while
Ignoring, a simple
Truth, "We're here
To lift humanity above
All."

In that
Context, mustn't we
Focus on well-being of
The whole; reaching
The mission we're here
To resolve it all?

Let
Freedom
Ring

Freedom
Is meaningful
Only

When we're
Awakened to our
Inglorious blunders
And sins

And, make
An earnest try to
Resolve 'em soon

Otherwise,
Guilt, grief and
Despair shall locked
Us in the cage for
A very long

Indeed,
The cage where
Our genuine freedom
Shall be questioned, and
Anguish would control
The mind…

En Route

Am I
Just an
Interpretive
Possibilities,

Or am I,
Another ordinary
Concrete experience
To be remembered

Am I still
Lost on the way
To discover my
Real path

Nothing
Is given but
Be earned and
That I try to know

Oh this existence
Wrapped by myriad
Antimonies; seeking my
Judgment every time…

Be
Inspired

Why
Pursue life to be
Told by others at
Every step of the way,
"How to live"

Why
Bow down to others
Always, who're not
Ready to listen,
"What you've to
Say in the matter"

I say,
"Rise up and be your
Confident self and voice
Your thoughts through
Smart actions"

Let the
World welcome you,
"As you're" and listen
What you've say in
The matter"

Let you enjoy
Freedom that you're
Entitled to since your
Arrival on the scene…"

Clarion
Bells

Why
Ignore the truth,
"We're here for a
While"

Why be
In souciant; knowing
"We're being stirred
Into this cauldron of
Uncertainty"

Isn't it
Time to acquire,
Unity of our collective
Awareness

Why don't
We expand our vision,
Our understanding of
One another, and of course,
Our gratitude to be alive

Time
To embattle the
Enemy within; saving
Our humanity at the core…

Message

We're
Connectivity between
Known and Unknown
In the totality of all that is

In such
A backdrop, wonder
How far have we evolved
As intelligent beings?

I mean,
"What have we learned,
But very erosion of
Our collective morality,
Dignity and integrity?"

Save for
A few impressive
Historic highlights and
Great innovations;

Still we've to enrich
Our humanity; ensuring a
Better world for our kids…

Unresolved

From this
Existential motif
To the realm beyond,

We the intelligent
Beings been asking
Many million questions

And yet the
Truth remains
Enigmatic

Is it the
Obstacle of our
Sheer ignorance

Is it the
Misread of the reality
We think know it well?

Come let us
Decipher the cause of
Our long time historic
Blunders and sins…

Twin
Wheels

Contextuality and
Choices must
Be the twin wheels;
Controlling destiny of
Every human we know

It's the
Interdependency of
Relationships and choices;
Defining our essence that
Sets the stage to seek
Beauty and Truth

Yes,
To strive for social
Validity, and explore
Endless possibilities

Oh yes,
Life is all about
Choices & relationships,
That very juice; ensuring
Our hope, harmony and
Happy feelings while
The ride is on…

Journey
Forever

In love
We shall keep dancing
'Till the end of the
Time

Yes,
Dear Soul let us
Keep enjoying through
The splendor of romance

Let us
Continue the
Magnifique journey of
Our souls together

I say,
"Let us just
Live in love forever"

Come
And let us
Begin the dance called,
"Two crazy lovers forever…"

The
Ladder

As earthly
Time keeps slowly
Slipping away

Human child
Evolves
From innocence
To experience
So soon

Thus to
Climb a ladder of
An intended maturity
And wisdom, if he's
Lucky!

Looking
Through the lenses
Of history, sadly only a
Few souls made it all
The way to wisdom, but
Why?

Transcendent

In these
Frozen moments
Of life, I am heading
Toward a higher realm

Still
Don't know, "Is it
My deep mediation or
The final flight?"

That only,
The death shall
Confirmed soon

As I am
Distancing from the
Earthly charm,
The soul is my only pal

That shall be
The complete closer
Of all my intended
Directions and

"Nothingness"
Shall be the final
Closer in the end…

Prognosis

Whenever
Humans forget their
Moral calls and fails
To regain integrity, evil
Begins to take hold

That is the
Lex unscripta, the
Unwritten
Law of Existence

That is the
Truth depicted by
World history over and
Again, and

The present is
Piggy-riding the past,
And who knows?

"What the future
Shall be the way
We humans been
Behaving lately?"

Time to Arise

Rescue
This human from
Drowning into the
Sea of struggles

Let
Inspiration and
Courage leads him
Through it all

Let him
Be free
Off the confined
Sphere; catapulting
To the larger world of
Vision

Let his
Noble mission be
A real opening, and
Let his
Freedom lifts him
Off the turbulent
Sea at last…

Evanescence

The
Other day,
I stopped by your
Place to say, "Hello"

And,
You didn't
Open the door

Thanks for
Ignoring the
Guy to whom

Once you
Welcomed him
With full-heart

Thought
You're sincere and
Brave and cared for
Our friendship

Still,
You haven't explained
And trying to hide the
Feelings, but why?

Return

Why be
A prisoner of
Your
Exclusiveness

When the
Whole world
Is enjoying,

All rhythms,
Melodies and
The beauty of
Being humans!

Why
Driven by myopia,
Phobia and anxiety,

When the
Whole world is
Ascending toward

Moral vision,
Honor and dignity
With great joy…

113

Birth of
A Hero

It's the
Awakened soul
That separates from
Others, and

Emerges
As the hero of a
Historic experience

It's the
Firmness of
"Goodwill"

That
Distinguishes a
Person from
Arrogant others

It's the
Strong Will that
Facilitates
Triumph over any
Challenge on the
Way...

One
Destiny

Our collective
Destiny is dependent
Upon what moral choices
We exercise

If they're
Sincere, there shall be
Stability, peace and
Order

If not,
We must keep
Relearning the lessons
From the dirty history

Where many
Great civilizations rose
And fell, time after time

Time to
Wake-up and take a
Firm stand

Time to
Understand the history
So-well and not to repeat
It time after time…

While
Here

Either
Super rich few or the
Struggling billions
All is
One in death and
There is no escape
Otherwise

That is the
Common destiny
To be aware at all
Times

While
Walking through the
Rough terrain, only
Self-confidence is the
Real friend

Let's
"Seize the day,
Seize the moment,
Seize the future for
Children to dream…"

Wisdom

Philosophy,
Always a challenging
Direction, "How to
Live with understanding
The self and the surrounding
World"

It's simply
A realm welcoming,
How to exercise reason
In evaluating and
Interpreting the widening
Human experiences including,
"How we ought to be?"

Philosophy,
"Always an inspiration,
"How to deepen vision,
Imaginations and
Determination; resolving,
Many unknowns; dwelling into
The inquisitive mind only!"

Mental
Gymnast

Being awakened
Is the very essence of
Human spirituality
In action

That is
Where he draws
His indomitable will
To explore

Yes,
To resolve great
Riddles, paradoxes and
Contradictions;

Turning
Them into
Simple logical steps;
From ignorance to the
Scintillating mind simply

May be, the
Mental gymnastics is
The best medicine while
Walking through the trail
Many unfolding meanings…

Glow in The Dark

Being
Alone
Is the unknown
Himself who's been
Challenged to be
Comprehend soon

He's the
Center to know the
Cosmic link

Let him
Be committed to
Make it through his
Noble mission

Being,
What a splendid
Universe of
Logic, ethics and
Moral will, indeed

Let him
Affirm individuality,
And let Him be the
Glow in the dark…

Time
To Act

In the totality
Of what I know,
Life be lived not for
A brief, but beyond

Yes,
Let every bold spirit
Understands either his
Madness or just a pure
Self-awareness!

Each is
Obliged to save his
Humanity and humanity
Of all others at the same
Time

That's the
Only way to let the
"Global Soul Speaking"

That's the
Only way to fulfill
All the waited dreams,
Today…

Recurrences

What if,
This reality is but
One profound
Ambiguity or what?

Where
Good and evil are
Intricately woven;
Expressing,

"Half 'n half
Pleasure and pain with
Different consequences,
Of course"

What if,
This corrupt mind is
The real interruption
To the journey of the
Sacred Soul;

Who's the
Genuine truth of all
Or what!

Spiritual Being

"All That is,"
Is the infinite sphere
Of my consciousness
To keep expanding
Forever

That is the
Direction where
Finite I and the Infinite
Have built the Holistic
Reality indeed

Yes,
That is where, only
The Eternal Essence
Shall remain as the
Nameless unknown

"All That is," is
The only sphere of
Human queries; keeping
His curiosity alive forever...

Point
Upward

To these
Symbols, their
Narratives and
Metaphors

All geared to
Awaken, man from
His deep slumber

And these
Myths, arts and all
Scientific endeavors;

Targeted,
To let him be a
Meaningful link between
"What is and what is not"

If that is
The essence of an
Intelligent being,
"Why then keeps
Drowning into tears and
Despair of his precious time?"

Karma

What was
Uttered yesterday
Is still true today

What was
The mode in
Seizing the power
Yesterday remains
Even today

What the
World suffered
Yesterday is doing
The same more or less,
Today

Though,
Humans changed
Many things, failed to
Change their very nature

Whence the past
Keeps chasing the present
And in turn, the present
Keeps shaping the future…

Fulfillment

Truth of
Existence is
Not about the divine,
But becoming an
Awakened soul

Life is
Not just about
Freedom, but taking
Responsibility to build
A better world

Religion,
If logical must
Strengthen,
"Good of the whole"

And, not stick
With it's confined
False narratives and
Myopic claims

Let
Our collective
Rational Enlightenment
Fulfill the best wishes
On our own…

Being & Freedom

What if
We ever encountered
A reality

Where living ones
Are dead and the dead
Being alive?

What if
All the geographically
Labeled gods roared
The deaf world,

"We're just the
Different manifests
Of the same; just to point
The right direction …"

What if,
All ignorant sheep's
Grasped such at simple truth,
I mean, "Will them return
To their renewed sanity or not?"

Human Intention

How far and
How long, do we keep
Stretching the thin
Thread while we're still
Unknown to the self

How long
Do we keep fighting
Anxieties and fear when
We're not willing to be
Fearless and self-confident
Ourselves

How long
Shall we keep triggering
Violence's, wars and genocides
In the name of uttered madness

It's the
World that is drowning
Into the sea of the seven
Sins, so our inglorious
Presence continues…

Reality, Blurred?

Every living
Human caught into
The moving storm of
Social and political
Constant change

In such a
Capricious turmoil,
Some end up being
Winners, and

Many keep
Struggling to get off
The deep hole

In that case,
We must ask,

"What is the
Validation of human
Justice, piety and
So on?"

I mean,
Preached in the name
Of the Unknown, who's
Known by different names!

Descendants

Let us
Hold
A clear crystal
Understanding,

"At times,
Life like war can
Instantly turn evil
In action"

Sorry,
That's the fact of
Historic experience
That's the work of
Our ancestors

Let us
Be awakened to the
Bloody past, and witness
What's happening in our
Time

Let us
Begin to give a damn,
Let's begin to get wise-up,
Let us think of our young…

Evolving Heroes

It's always
That universal saga
Man and woman;
Falling in love and
Soon after turning
Rivals to dominate
The scene

In the old days,
It was misogynistic
Male who called the shots;
Reducing her dignity to
Nothing

It was in the
Humiliating past, male
Controlled slavery, trade and
Parasitic policies to exploit
The helpless

In modern time,
Oppressed people still
Resisting injustice, and
The beat goes on…

Gauntlet

We may arrive
A wise conclusion,
"Existence without a
Moral essence and lack
Of Self knowledge means
We're no better than the
Worms."

Even
The spider in a
Complex web knows,
"How to turn its existence
Into meaning, all right"

Oh yes,
Those countless stars;
Offering meaning through
Illuminating the darkness,
Every where

The issue being,
"When the intelligent being
Is going to roll-up the sleeves
And move the mountains,
Once again!"

Empathy

Being
Owners of our
Individual precious
Humanity

We must
Be stirred by the
Humiliation of any part
Of the whole, what is a total
Humanity, indeed

Every
Dying human in a
War, violence or from
Hunger is a sinful assault
On us all

Let us
Begin to soften-up,
Let us
Reckon, we're all
One,

Let us
Learn to see in their
Misery and as our own…

Journey Ahead

Let the ideas
Flow,
Let ambitions
Grow and
Let humans
Continue to glow

Time to
Purify the mind
Time to
Look beyond,
Time to
Walk the walk

Let each
Succeed in their
Quest of spiritual
Worthiness, and

Let each
Probe,
"What be his/her
Moral responsibility
To lift this desperate
World?"

Off the Track

Let's
Understand,
"There is no death,

Only
Incessant flow
Of genes from one
Generation to the next"

There is
No fear to the soul,
But to the emotional
Being only

There is
No unknown to the
Awakened, but to
The capricious mind
Simply

There is
No need of divine
To the moral braves, only
For the fearful weak...

Give
A Damn

In every
Age, folks must
Come to a covenant,

"It's better to
Take a moral stand
Together against injustice
Instead dying alone in
Silent rage"

In our
Age, folks must also
Come to a covenant,

"It's the time
To stand together with
One voice; demanding
Resolution to threat from
Nukes, climate change and
Super smart machines"

Folks, it's
High noon,
We tackle together,
Destabilizing forces:
Violence's, wars and
Gluttony of greed, today...

It's the
Attitude

When
A person's life
Is nothing but lies,

What is
The point, keep
Falling into such a
Hellish pit?

When
A person is under
A great stress,

"Why doesn't
He seek calm with
Some intelligent
Choice?"

When
A person is walking
Through the dark,

"Why doesn't
He looks at the stars
Above and be inspired!"

Wild
Card

Man
Shall gain great
Knowledge via
Multiple quests

But, the
Irrational in him
May well be the
Hidden variable;

Undermining
All his endeavors
Toward wisdom

That's been
The lingering wild
Card through history
And stays active today

Most everything,
Changed from one
Geographic God to
Another, but the basic
Human nature hasn't…

Rides,
On

We're
Brave warriors
Caught into
Our moral conflict,
Day in and day out

That is
The unspoken
Existence; albeit a
Silent reality, today

Humans,
Always a glowing
Gems of their "Rights
And wrongs"

If so, why they
Don't take a bold
Stand demanding,

"Why not
Change the age old
Destructive habits, and
Live in the world as it
Ought to be."

Be
Informed

These
False values,
Myopic visions and
Techno- addictions

Not leading
Us to the world of
Illumination

No point,
Slumbering and
Not responding to
Devil in-making

Think smart,
"What's happening
To our rich heritage,
Family integrity and
Humanity today?"

Future,
Now

Every human
Is the cause and consequence
Of social and cultural implications

Every human
Is the creator of either good or bad;
Often letting others to pay for it;
Directly or indirectly,
Of course

If every human,
Is aware of his/her moral goodwill
And got a cooperative spirit; there
Shall be sovereignty of "Good,"
Always of course

Let the
Children be taught such
Simple lessons, and groom them
Accordingly to build a world of
Harmony, unlike their elders,
Of course…

Covenant

Now that
Our immersion into
The honey bud is over

Dear lady,
"How shall we learn,
To resolve our differences
That has just begun?"

Yes, our time
Flew by too soon, but
The light of love still
Is on

Let's
Define from this point
On, "How do we stay
As one with deep trust and
The sense of forgiveness?"

Yes dear heart,
"How do we continue
The journey from here
To eternity; sustaining our
Strong friendship."

The Blueprint

In the naked
Reality, no one is a
Complete sovereign, but
Must willing to cooperate

That's
Why spiritual teachings
And rational insights play
Pertinent part

Yes, to
Strengthen the moral
Will of the whole
Yes, for the
Survival of the whole

That's
Why all responsible
Religions must be geared
Toward unifying the
"Global Goodwill"

That is the
Pragmatic passage to
Transcend from hellish to the
Heavenly state of the mind…

Thought & Reality

While the
Mighty universe is
Going from one cycle
Another

Will life
Too enter another
Reality or what?

While
Humanity is silently
Dying here,
How certain
Should we be of our
Identity?

All seems
In eternal flux, and
All is a cyclical creation,
Explosion and rebirth

All seems,
Build-up thoughts of
The conscious being…

Declaration

Caught by the
Worldly turmoil,
Is it not time to resolve
The collective sin from
The Past

The past
That imposes it's
Heavy burden upon
The Present

Why not then
Set the Present on a
Different track, and
Be the guarantors of
A happy future

Why don't
We stand-up and
Declare our intention
To the deaf world,

"End this
Dark necessity of
Violence and war, and
Get on the right track……"

Be
Fearless

Why we
Mortals
Keep struggling
From birth to the
Noble death?

Why don't
We be strong will
To be winners while
Journeying in-between
Them

Why we
Mortals don't dare to
Be the heroes in the
Stated game, and
Why be obsessed with
The fear of noble death!

Hello Mr. Obscure

Man, aka
Mr. Obscure lying
Along the flowing
Stream

He kept
Counting; how many
Flowers passed by yet
Unable to pick any in
His time

Suddenly,
He realized his
Missing identity as his
Name never appeared
In any census

Mr. Obscure
Experienced his non-
Existential status for the
First time

He understood,
He was the face of
Many billions; sleeping
On the streets, called,
"Dead Souls."

Take
Note

Yesterday,
Birds sang their
Sweet songs

Well, today is
No different, but
The clock ticks on

In other words,
Reality
Doesn't change,
But the time does

I mean, reality
Doesn't disappear,
But humanity does

That's why
"Societal triumph"
Must be a top priority

Or the
Evil doers shall
Set up the "Societal
Failure for sure…"

Big
Charade

Often we
Wonder, "If this
Existence is a mere
Mirage or what?"

What if
It's a metaphysical
Melodramatic brief
Experience or what?

And, what if
In the totality of all
That is, we're simply
Projected images on the
Holographic screen!

What if,
"We're the evanescent
Events; never knowing
What's the meaning of
Our births and deaths in
This big charade?"

Secret of Life

Life
Ain't a process of
Decay, but a hopeful
Rejuvenation of the
Moral spirit

Life
Ain't senseless
Milieu filled with
Violence and
Myopic claims of the
Mad-dog zealots

Instead, it's
A beautiful garden of
Noble thoughts and
Actions

Let's
Validate life as
An enlightened mind

Let it be a
Sharpe jolt for the
Deep slumbering
Human himself…

One
Direction

No point
In beating around the bush
By delivering false promises
To the innocent masses when
Needing their votes

No point
In punishing the millions
Struggling middle class
By exporting their livelihoods
Elsewhere

After all,
They are the pillars of
Successful democracy and
A definite unity of it all

Let there
Be rational and a moral
Balance between"Have-ones
And have-nots"

Let each
Participate with deeper
Understanding and the value
Of our common destiny at
This critical point of our time…

Transition

It was
Once believed,
"Man's fate is
Decided by is
God"

Today,
The illumined
Mind affirms
Otherwise

"It's the
Revolving
Thoughts and
Choices and set
Circumstances;
Governing his
Journey all right…"

In modern
Time, it's also the
Super smart thinking
Machines, emerging as the
"Nova Techno God" and
They got the godly power
Judge his fate too!

Magic,
Simply

Love,
What a sweet and
Sour human experience,
While being on the road to
Their waiting dream

Love,
Always a double-edged
Sword hanging over the
Heads of crazy lovers at
All times

Love,
What a great challenge;
Measuring the depth of
Commitment, trust and
Sacrifice of two throbbing
Hearts…

Don't
Wait

Let us
Be aware, our
Individual dignity
Should never be
Crushed by anyone

Let us
Be on the guard that
No one dare throw us
Off the set track

Let us
Never fail to defend
Our precious humanity
And humanity of others,
If evil forces make their
Moves

Let us
Learn to take
Responsibility to secure
A better future for our
Kids and

Of course,
Those of others too;
Only then we shall all
Coexist in the reality of peace...

Meditation

Why
When one mind of a
Given belief enters
Another;
They're frightened?

Why
When one enters the realm
Of another's cultural identity,
They're fearful?

Why
Everyone seeks to
Propagate their narratives
While ignoring, or even
Dehumanizing the others?

In this
Age of information,
"Why paradoxically still
Be ignorant, arrogant
And being indifferent?"

JAGDISH J. BHATT, PhD

Brings 45 years of academic experience including a post-doctorate research scientist at Stanford University, CA. His total career publications: scientific, educational and literary is 100 including 60 books.

Made in the USA
Columbia, SC
19 August 2023

21810011R00085